Making Grizzle Grow

To every kid who has Growled and Grizzled
-Rachna

For my father, David Watts, who read to me every night
-Leslie

Text copyright © 2007 by Rachna Gilmore
Illustration copyright © 2007 by Leslie Elizabeth Watts

Published in Canada by Fitzhenry & Whiteside, 195 Allstate Parkway, Markham, Ontario L3R 4T8

Published in the United States by Fitzhenry & Whiteside, 311 Washington Street, Brighton, Massachusetts 02135

www.fitzhenry.ca   godwit@fitzhenry.ca

10 9 8 7 6 5 4 3 2 1

Library and Archives Canada Cataloguing in Publication
Gilmore, Rachna, 1953-
Making Grizzle grow / Rachna Gilmore ; illustrated by Leslie Elizabeth Watts.
ISBN 978-1-55041-885-9
1. Dilophosaurus-Juvenile fiction. I. Watts, Leslie Elizabeth, 1961- II. Title.
PS8563.I57M34 2007   jC813'.54   C2007-902284-7

**U.S. Publisher Cataloging-in-Publication Data
(Library of Congress Standards)**

Gilmore, Rachna., 1953-

Making Grizzle grow / Rachna Gilmore ; illustrated by Leslie Elizabeth Watts.
[32] p. : col. ill.. ;   cm.

Summary: When Dad doesn't have time to play in the snow with her, Emily is annoyed.
Then she becomes so mad that she makes a snow dinosaur and calls it Grizzle. Grizzle
comes alive, and she is a Dilophosaurus with a temper to match Emily's.

ISBN- 13: 978-1-55041-885-9

1. Fathers and daughters — Fiction - Juvenile literature.
I. Watts, Leslie Elizabeth, 1961- II. Title.
[E] dc22 PZ7.G556 M 2007

 **Canada Council   Conseil des Arts
for the Arts   du Canada**

ONTARIO ARTS COUNCIL
CONSEIL DES ARTS DE L'ONTARIO

Fitzhenry & Whiteside acknowledges with thanks the Canada Council for the Arts, and the
Ontario Arts Council for their support of our publishing program. We acknowledge
the financial support of the Government of Canada through the Book Publishing
Industry Development Program (BPIDP) for our publishing activities.

Design by Wycliffe Smith Design Inc.

Making Grizzle Grow

by

Rachna Gilmore

Illustrated by

Leslie Elizabeth Watts

F i t z h e n r y   &   W h i t e s i d e

Later! It's always later. Dad
promised he'd make snow
animals with me. But now
he has to work.

"I'll come when I'm done,
Emily," he says.

I don't even look at him.
I yank on my snowsuit.

"I'm sorry, Emily," says
Dad, in his I-know-you'll-
understand voice. "But I
have to sort this out."

I stomp outside and
slam the door shut.

The backyard glitters with
snow. It's thick and lonely.

Dad sits by the window
and waves to me, wearing his
best-buddies grin.

Who needs him? I can
make a better animal without
him. A much better animal.

Something big.

I make a dinosaur. She's amazing! She has a huge head with sharp, hungry teeth. She's a Dilophosaurus. Her name is **Grizzle**.

Dad opens the window.

"Hey, that's a cute little animal, Emily."

Cute?

Little!

Grizzle rumbles deep inside her throat.

"Don't worry, **Grizzle**." I scowl. "I'll help you grow."

I scoop together snow and make a huge stack of pizzas. Double pepperoni and cheese. No olives or anchovies—no icky stuff Dad likes.

Grizzle snaps her teeth. One bite and the pizzas are gone.

Grizzle is bigger. A grown-up Dilophosaurus. She looks at the window and tosses her head. But Dad's busy working. He doesn't even notice.

"**More**," huffs **Grizzle**.

I cook up a mound of hot dogs.
Cheeseburgers with the works. Monster
meatballs with spaghetti.

Grizzle snorts. One gulp
and the food is gone.

Grizzle is waaay bigger.
A Megalosaurus.

She flashes her teeth at
the window. But Dad

just stares at his work and scratches
his nose. I bet he's picking it, even
though *I'm* not allowed 'cause
it's too disgusting.

"**More!**" growls **Grizzle**.

I rush around and make a mountain of steaks. A humongous roast turkey. Pots of burning-hot chili.

One crunch and the food disappears.

I make sweet-and-sour spareribs. Beef sausages. Piles of pork chops.

Grizzle crams it all down.

She's huge now, especially around her mouth and teeth. And claws.

But still **Grizzle** snarls, "MORE!"

I push my hair off my face. My arms are sore. I'm hot and sweaty.

Maybe…maybe **Grizzle**'s big enough now. She's an Allosaurus. She's already a lot bigger than I am.

Grizzle grinds her teeth and snaps. So I throw together some Brussels sprouts and zucchini. Tossed salad with low-fat cottage cheese—the stuff Dad eats when he's trying to lose weight. **Grizzle** just scarfs it down.

"MORE!" she roars.

I'm not going to argue with an Allosaurus. Especially one with stinky breath. So I scrape together some boring old snow porridge.

As fast as I bring it, **Grizzle** gobbles it down. She's e**NOR**mous. But still she booms, "**MORE!**"

I lean against my shovel. "But…but, there's hardly any snow left."

Grizzle opens her mouth wide. She picks her teeth with a wicked claw. She's a Tyrannosaurus rex now. I don't think she's too big on listening.

I try to laugh, to show we're still friends. "N-nice **Grizzle**," I say. I edge away from her mouth. "Niiiice **Grizzley**." "**MORE!**" thunders **Grizzle**.

Dad opens the back door. "Hey, Emily! Want some hot chocolate?"

Grizzle drools. Her stomach rumbles.

"Wow! That's really something," says Dad, staring at **Grizzle**.

He smiles and comes down the steps. Dad's awfully small compared to **Grizzle**. And his shirt isn't tucked in, so his belly shows.

I know he can't run in those slippers.

"Goody!" croaks **Grizzle**.
"**MO-ORE!**"

For a moment
I just stand there.
Frozen.

Then I scream,
"NO! Watch out, Dad! I'll save you!"
I dive into **Grizzle**. She twists and
turns, her snowy teeth flashing. But I grab
her and grab her till she's smushed to the
ground.

Dad comes running and holds me tight.

Grizzle is gone! There's just a pile of snow where she used to be.

"Are you all right?" asks Dad, picking up his slippers.

I nod. I'm only shivering because it's so cold.

Inside, on the kitchen table, is a steaming mug of hot chocolate. With two marshmallows. And my favorite ginger cookies.

Dad pulls on dry socks. "Thanks for saving me, Emily."

I sip my hot chocolate and nod carelessly. "It's nothing, Dad. It was just an old snow dinosaur."

Dad smiles, his eyes all soft and mushy. "Okay if I come out with you now?"

I try not to grin, but one side of my mouth turns up all by itself.

Dad gets me dry mittens. We go outside together.

"All right," I say, crunching my excellent cookie. "You pick what we make."

"Mmm. How about a Tyrannosaurus rex?"

"No!" I shake my head. "Not a Tyrannosaurus rex. No way a Tyrannosaurus rex! Definitely not a Tyrannosaurus rex!"

"Okay," says Dad. "Then what?"

"A Brachiosaurus."

"Why a Brachiosaurus?"